THE TALE OF

Tuppence
and Tiffany

For Jonathan, Peter and Amy

Text copyright © 1990 Pat Wynnejones
Illustrations copyright © 1990 Sheila Ratcliffe

Published by
Lion Publishing plc
Sandy Lane West, Oxford, England
ISBN 0 7459 1947 2
Lion Publishing Corporation
1705 Hubbard Avenue, Batavia, Illinois 60510, USA
ISBN 0 7459 1947 2
Albatross Books Pty Ltd
PO Box 320, Sutherland, NSW 2232, Australia
ISBN 0 7324 0229 8

First edition 1991

British Library Cataloguing in Publication Data
(Applied for)

Library of Congress Cataloging in Publication Data
(Applied for)

Printed and bound in Singapore

THE TALE OF
Tuppence and Tiffany

Retold by Pat Wynnejones
from Mrs Gatty's 'Parables from Nature'

Illustrated by Sheila Ratcliffe

A LION BOOK

Oxford · Batavia · Sydney

It was winter. The countryside was deep in snow, but in
a corner of the manor house kitchen Taffeta, a silky
tabby cat with white paws and tummy, was warm and
comfortable. Tucked up close beside her in her basket
was her newborn kitten, Tiffany, pure white except for
her nose, which was pink, and her eyes, which were
blue, though we could not have told, for they were tight
closed.

Ting-a-ling! Ting-a-ling! Someone was jangling the
bell outside the kitchen door. Martha, the cook, looked
up from her pastry, wiped the flour from her hands,
tutting with irritation, and opened the door, letting in a
snow flurry. Tom, the gardener's boy, was standing
there.

'Oh, Tom, it's you! Come in, lad, and close the door
quick.' Tom came in, dripping snowy puddles on the red
tiles.

'Tom! Tom! What are you doing, you thoughtless
boy! Just look at those muddy footmarks all over my
nice clean floor! Well, well, never mind. Come sit by the
fire, lad, and warm yourself. But what have you got
there?'

For Tom was carrying something under his coat.

Slowly and carefully Tom opened his shabby jacket enough to show a tiny, frozen, half dead black kitten, not much older than Tiffany, with muddy fur and a bloody injured paw.

'Oh, my goodness gracious, wherever did you get that?'

'I found it in the potting shed, ma'am. How it got there I don't know. But Ma won't let me have it at home. She says she's got enough to feed and care for, what with five of us and the new baby. So – so I brought it here, ma'am, to you. I couldn't leave it to die.'

'Well, Tom, you did the right thing, bless you. Poor little mite! Leave it to die in the snow? I should think not! Goodness gracious me! I should think not indeed!'

Martha reached up to the mantelpiece, took down a Toby jug, tipped it up and shook out two bright shining pennies.

'There, Tom. There's tuppence for you, for being a good kind lad and caring for one of God's creatures. Just keep the little tuppenceworth of trouble warm while I pop my pie in the oven, and we'll see what we can do to clean her up.'

While this was going on Taffeta was watching from her warm corner. She saw Tom hold the feeble little creature while cook bathed the hurt paw and cleaned the muddy fur. Small and weak though it was, she saw the kitten stretch out its other paw to give Tom a quick scratch.

'There's gratitude for you', thought Taffeta. 'That's what comes of bringing strangers in – you don't know where they've been, or what they're like, or how they will turn out.'

But her mothering instinct was strong and she didn't object when without a 'by your leave' or a 'please may I?' Martha popped the little stranger into the basket beside Tiffany saying, 'There, you've got enough milk for two. It won't hurt you to give a little to "Tuppence" here.'

So 'Tuppence' became the new kitten's name, and out of the kindness of her heart Taffeta took her as her own and raised her along with Tiffany.

However, the two kittens were very different. Tiffany had a happy nature and purred when she was pleased, which was most of the time, but Tuppence was wild and scared and never purred.

They had been licked all over, hundreds of times, by the same warm tongue, given the same advice, slept in the same basket, yet never were two kittens more thoroughly unlike than those two. Tiffany, with an open loving heart, purred her friendship to all the world; Tuppence, who never purred, was more than likely to scratch.

Rupert, who lived at the manor house, loved to play with the kittens. Every morning, when he brought them a saucer of milk, Tiffany would thank him with a gentle little rumbling purr in her throat, but Tuppence would drink hers silently and dart away.

Sometimes he would tie a string with a cork at the end of it to the handle of the kitchen table drawer, so they could paw and pat and spring at it as they pleased, but it was always Tiffany who seemed to be enjoying herself most. And if there was nothing else, there was always her own tail to chase, to make Rupert laugh.

But if he approached Tuppence she would hide behind the coal-scuttle and spit.

'Why do *you* never make me laugh?' asked Rupert, picking up Tuppence gently, so that he could look into her eyes. But there was no response except a movement of her tiny tail, which said quite definitely that she wished to be put down.

One day Tiffany plucked up her courage and boldly asked Tuppence, 'Why do you *never* purr? Why don't you like to play or be stroked or cuddled?'

Tuppence was very taken aback by the question and did not know what to answer, but at last she said sadly, 'I don't know. I only know that there's a hard sort of feeling inside me.'

A few days before Christmas Rupert's cousin, Bethany, came to stay. She was about the same age as Rupert, but as different from him in her nature as Tuppence was from Tiffany. Rupert was mischievous, full of fun and laughter, while Bethany was pale and solemn.

For the strangely quiet little girl had been an orphan for nearly two years, her parents having been killed in an accident. She had never cried, but ever since she had withdrawn into her shell and never smiled.

Good-natured Rupert did his best to make his guest happy, sharing his toys and thinking of games to play. But she only responded to his efforts in the same unmoved, uninterested tone in which she always spoke.

On Christmas Eve Rupert's mother told the children that they would each be allowed to choose a kitten to call their very own.

Taffeta was carefully washing the two kittens, licking them thoroughly from ears to toes, when Rupert burst into the kitchen followed by his silent cousin.

'Come on, Beth,' he was saying, 'they're going to give us the kittens for our very own. Which do you want? You choose first.'

Now as soon as Beth had set eyes on the shy wild black kitten her heart had gone out to her, and she had longed to befriend her.

'Oh, Rupert,' she cried, her eyes shining, 'please may I have the sad one, the one that never purrs? I'll love her and I'll make her happy.'

Rupert was delighted. He had unselfishly let Beth choose first, but it was Tiffany that he had always wanted for his own.

After church on Christmas Day Rupert went riding with his father, while Beth took Tuppence up to the schoolroom by herself. She was glad to be on her own with the kitten, to cuddle her and gain her confidence when no one else was near, comforting her with gentle words born out of her own sorrow.

So it was that her aunt, coming suddenly into the room, discovered her kneeling by the sofa, weeping a positive rain of tears over the small black fur bundle that she held tightly in her arms, and that was actually beginning to make a faint little purring sound.

'Oh, my darling,' cried her aunt, hurrying to take Beth on her lap, 'that's right – cry all you want. That's the best thing you could do.'

'Oh, Auntie,' sobbed Beth through her tears, 'I'm not crying for myself, but for Tuppence. She has lost her parents, like me, so I know just how she feels. She has been too sad to purr and too unhappy to play. But now, listen, she's just beginning to purr!'

As her aunt's arms folded round Beth a sense of comforting tenderness crept into her lonely heart. Gradually her sobs ceased as she stroked her kitten, who quite soon was sleeping peacefully in the warmth and safety of her love.

'You see, Auntie,' whispered Beth, with the glimmer of a truly happy smile, 'Tuppence knows that I understand her!'

That evening Rupert's father gave each of the kittens a present from the Christmas Tree – a soft ball on elastic, blue for Tiffany, and red for Tuppence. The kittens sprang for them as the children dangled them up and down.

Taffeta was watching from the window-seat. 'Well, well,' she mewed. 'That's a change! Tuppence is playing quite as happily as Tiffany!'

The four stories in 'Village Tales' have been re-created from Mrs Gatty's 'Parables from Nature', first published in 1855. Mrs Gatty was a children's writer, and also a keen naturalist, who used stories from the world of nature to illustrate and communicate truths about God and his purposes. Each of the stories has a particular theme, based on a verse from the Bible.

In these modern versions, the stories have lost none of their original freshness and charm, and their message is as relevant today as when they were first written.

'The Tale of Tuppence and Tiffany' is about compassion, passing on the comfort of God's love to others. The story is based on the words of Paul in his letter to the Christians at Corinth: 'God comforts us in all our troubles, so that we in turn may be able to comfort others in any trouble of theirs' (2 Corinthians 1:4).